Super powers

Stolen dogs

Hidden clues

Thief

Mystery

Locked doors

D1328888

Pete Johnson is a bestselling author for children and teenagers. His books have been translated into twelve different languages, and he has won a number of prizes, including the Sheffield Children's Book Award and the Calderdale Children's Book of the Year.

He was inspired to become a writer by Dodie Smith. He wrote her a fan letter, at the age of ten, after reading *The Hundred and One Dalmatians*. They went on to write to each other for many years.

Pete thinks the best time for writing is first thing in the morning and he likes to get started by 7 a.m. Whenever he is stuck he takes his mad King Charles spaniel, Tilly, for a very long walk.

Books by Pete Johnson

2-POWER: THE KORSKI CODE
2-POWER: THE CANINE CONSPIRACY

PIRATE BROTHER

For older readers

THE COOL BOFFIN
THE EX-FILES
FAKING IT
THE HERO GAME

PETE JOHNSON

Illustrations by Rowan Clifford

PUFFIN

PUFFIN BOOKS

Published by the Penguin Group
Penguin Books Ltd, 80 Strand, London WC2R ORL, England
Penguin Group (USA) Inc., 375 Hudson Street, New York, New York 10014, USA
Penguin Group (Canada), 90 Eglinton Avenue East, Suite 700, Toronto, Ontario, Canada M4P 2Y3
(a division of Pearson Penguin Canada Inc.)
Penguin Ireland, 25 St Stephen's Green, Dublin 2, Ireland (a division of Penguin Books Ltd)
Penguin Group (Australia), 250 Camberwell Road, Camberwell, Victoria 3124, Australia
(a division of Pearson Australia Group Pty Ltd)
Penguin Books India Pvt Ltd, 11 Community Centre, Panchsheel Park,
New Delhi – 110 017, India
Penguin Group (NZ), 67 Apollo Drive, Rosedale, North Shore 0632, New Zealand
(a division of Pearson New Zealand Ltd)
Penguin Books (South Africa) (Pty) Ltd, 24 Sturdee Avenue, Rosebank,
Johannesburg 2196, South Africa

Penguin Books Ltd, Registered Offices: 80 Strand, London WC2R ORL, England

puffinbooks.com

First published 2007
1

Text copyright © Pete Johnson, 2007
Illustrations copyright © Rowan Clifford, 2007
All rights reserved

The moral right of the author and illustrator has been asserted

Set in Bembo
Typeset by Palimpsest Book Production Ltd, Grangemouth, Stirlingshire
Made and printed in England by Clays Ltd, St Ives plc

British Library Cataloguing in Publication Data
A CIP catalogue record for this book is available from the British Library

ISBN: 978-0-141-32001-4

Contents

The Magic Begins

'Oh no! We're going to be very late,' cried Ella, rushing to the door.

'Who cares,' replied Sam, her twin brother, strolling after her. 'Oh, but I forgot, perfect Ella is *never* late for school . . . why, you might even get told off for the first time in your life.'

'I've been told off at school before,' said Ella.

'When?' demanded Sam.

'I can't remember exactly.'

Sam laughed. 'Anyway, it's your fault we're late. You spent about ten years saying goodbye to Patch.'

Patch was an abandoned dog who they'd discovered in a terrible condition. They'd taken him to the vet but no one had claimed him and now Patch belonged to them.

'It's just he hates to see us go,' said Ella. 'Aunt Joy complained that he howled for twenty minutes after we left yesterday.'

'And wouldn't *you* howl,' replied Sam, 'knowing you had to spend the rest of the day with those two ghastly crones?'

Sam and Ella's parents were dead and they'd been sent to live with Uncle Mike and Aunt Joy, who ran a little hotel by the sea called the Jolly Roger. Ella and Sam loved living by the seaside in Little Brampton, but they hated all the chores their uncle and aunt made them do. Every day the twins had to wash hundreds of dishes and clean the guests' rooms.

'Uncle Mike was really moaning about Patch yesterday,' said Ella. 'He said what a nuisance he was – and how his howling annoys the guests. You don't think he'll make us get rid of Patch, do you?'

'I'll punch him if he does,' said Sam so fiercely that he made Ella laugh.

Then she looked at her watch again. 'We're going to be really, really late now.'

Sam gazed at her. 'There is one way we can still get there on time . . .'

Ella smiled and a tingle of excitement ran through her.

She and Sam shared a magical secret. When they both concentrated hard they could actually hear each other's thoughts. So Ella could be far away from Sam and still hear his voice inside her right ear. They could chat away for ages without anyone ever knowing. Whenever they had one of their secret conversations they called it 'going online'. And recently they had made an incredible discovery.

When they were online together they stopped being ordinary. All at once they had special powers. For a start, they were mega strong — able to lift really heavy objects without blinking an eye. They had incredible hearing, and all their other senses were much sharper too.

Sam declared once, 'We've turned into superheroes!' and that's exactly what it felt like. But the moment they stopped being online their special powers vanished instantly.

Ella was as thrilled by this discovery as Sam. But she was also eight minutes older than him and always saw herself as the sensible one. She knew they must keep their super powers hidden, for if Uncle Mike and Aunt Joy ever discovered their secret, they'd do something really horrible – like allow people to do loads of experiments on them.

So Ella was always trying to stop Sam showing off. Still, if they ran to school along the seafront when hardly anyone was about yet, that should be all right.

She smiled at Sam and said, 'Come on then. Let's have some fun.'

Luckily the Jolly Roger was just across the road from the beach. It was a bright morning and the sea gleamed and flashed in the sunshine.

Ella took a deep breath. The air smelt so strongly of seaweed she could almost taste it. Then she closed her eyes tight. This was how she started going online. She began picturing Sam in her head, with his silly grin and hair that always looked a mess, even when he'd just combed it.

And then . . . Ella always thought there should be a burst of light when the magic was about to begin. But nothing like that happened. Instead, sometimes her nose started to twitch as if she were just about to sneeze. And then there came a funny buzzing noise, which meant you were getting through. And just a couple of seconds later Sam's voice rang out in her ear, although his mouth didn't move at all.

'Hello, Freckles.' He said that deliberately because he knew she HATED every one of her million freckles.

'Hello, most annoying brother in the entire universe,' she replied.

Then a little shiver ran through her as she realized she wasn't poor little Ella any more, who got a stitch after she'd run a few metres and came last in every one of her races. She'd changed into someone incredibly powerful and strong. No wonder everything looked extra bright now.

'Shall we go for a run then?' asked Sam.

'Oh yes,' said Ella.

And they didn't run – they *flew* along that seafront.

'This is the only way to travel,' said Sam.

'We're going so fast,' replied Ella, 'yet I don't feel the least bit out of breath.'

'And normally you have to rest if you run down the stairs,' teased Sam.

The beach was practically deserted at this time of the morning, save for some seagulls swooping and screaming above their heads – and old Tom, the beach treasure hunter. He was already out with his metal detector and he called after Ella and Sam: 'What on earth have you two had for breakfast? Never seen anyone move so fast!'

'Oh, we're world-champion runners – didn't you know?' boasted Sam as he surged past old Tom. 'Look out for us on the telly.'

'Will you stop showing off,' cried Ella.

'I'm not. I bet we really could be champions at the speed we're going right now.'

And they'd raced along so fast they actually arrived at school three minutes early. As they came through the school gates Sam looked back. With his mega hearing he'd just picked up something. He saw by Ella's face that she'd caught it too: a dog yelping in fear. Tiny little cries that even somebody nearby wouldn't have heard. Only Sam and Ella, online, could have detected those sounds.

'It sounds very frightened,' said Ella. 'Poor little dog.'

'How do you know what size it is?' demanded Sam.

'It just sounds little,' replied Ella.

And then they heard it again: a tiny yelp that even their magnified hearing only just picked up.

'We've got to find it,' murmured Ella.

Sam nodded. 'The sound is coming from the park . . . let's go.'

A Terrible Discovery

The park was just down the road from their school, so Sam and Ella reached it very quickly. One part was very popular with dog owners, for here they could let their pets off the lead to play ball or just tear about madly.

An Alsatian was being trained by its owner: 'Sit. No, sit,' cried the woman, while the Alsatian just stood staring at her. But then Sam and Ella heard a voice they recognized.

'Oh, come on, Spike! Where are you?'

'That's Lauren's voice,' said Ella. They knew Lauren had a corgi called Spike. Sam and Ella had never actually seen him but they'd heard how lively and friendly he was. Lauren and her dad were peering in all the hedges and bushes at the top of the park. Ella and Sam charged over to them.

'We can't find Spike anywhere,' Lauren wailed when she saw them.

'What happened?' asked Sam.

'We were playing ball with Spike, as we always do before school, when I got a call on Dad's mobile,' said Lauren. 'It was my nan ringing to wish me happy birthday –' she gave a little gasp, '– and suddenly we couldn't see Spike. We thought he was just off having a sniff around somewhere, so I've been calling and calling him – he always comes when he hears me – but he's vanished.'

'He's just gone off after a rabbit,' said Lauren's dad firmly. 'He'll turn up.'

'Of course he will,' said Sam. 'He wouldn't want to miss your birthday.' Lauren managed a weak smile at that. 'Don't worry, we'll find him for sure,' Sam went on.

Lauren and her dad continued to rush around the park calling Spike's name, while Sam and Ella searched through the undergrowth. Of course they stayed online. Suddenly Sam's extra-strong sense of smell picked something up.

He crouched down and found – a

piece of meat. The meat had string tied on to it. *Had this been used to lure Spike away, where someone pounced on him?* Sam shuddered.

'Oh no.' Ella was standing beside Sam now, looking really upset. 'Do you think someone's stolen Spike?'

Sam didn't answer as Lauren had joined them, looking pale and scared. Lauren pointed at the meat, and then let out a cry of horror.

'Oh, my poor Spike,' she gasped.

Where is Spike?

Lauren didn't turn up for lessons until the middle of the morning, and the class had been told not to bother her with lots of questions. So Ella and Sam just smiled sympathetically at the red-eyed girl, who couldn't eat a single thing at lunchtime.

At the end of school Lauren's mum and dad both turned up. They wanted to have a talk with her class.

Lauren's dad told them Spike had still not been found. There were groans of disbelief from everyone. 'So I'm afraid it does look as if Spike has been stolen,' said Lauren's dad. 'We do have one important clue, though.'

Everyone leant forward. 'The park keeper, Mr Westbury, saw a man leave the park at around the time Spike disappeared. Mr Westbury noticed this man because he was wearing a very bulky brown jacket on such a warm day. He was walking briskly and he didn't get into a car, just went on down the road.'

'I bet he had poor little Spike hidden inside his jacket,' Sam whispered to Ella. 'That's the dog snatcher all right.' Then he asked out loud, 'Can Mr Westbury describe this man at all?'

'Well, Mr Westbury, who's been very helpful, says he didn't get a good look at him, especially as he left so quickly. All he can tell us is that he was bald and very tall.' Lauren's dad added, 'We're going to find this dog thief.'

Everyone cheered then.

Lauren's mum spoke next. 'We've already contacted our vet. She said it was a shame Spike hadn't been microchipped. It only takes a few seconds and is a good way of identifying your pet. So, if you haven't microchipped your dog yet, please think about doing so, to keep him safe.' Her voice fell away for a moment. But then she said, 'Spike has got a blue collar with his name and our address and telephone number on. We've also

contacted the police and the lost-dog
website, and we've made some posters.'
She held one up, which read:

WHERE IS SPIKE NOW?

Underneath was a picture of Spike and
then:

PLEASE HELP US FIND
OUR DOG.
HE WENT MISSING
FROM TEMPLE PARK
AT 8.40 A.M. ON MONDAY.

There followed some more details
about who to contact. And it ended by
saying:

WE MISS SPIKE TERRIBLY AND
WANT HIM SAFE WITH US
AGAIN, SO PLEASE KEEP A
LOOKOUT FOR HIM.
THANK YOU VERY MUCH.

'We'd be so grateful,' said Lauren's
mum, 'if you could put these posters
up in the window of your house and
give some to neighbours and
friends . . .'

Sam took a huge pile of posters. 'We'll
stick them up all over the hotel,' he said.

'That's very kind of you,' said Lauren's
mum.

Then Sam looked at Lauren. Her lip
was quivering and she was trying hard
not to cry. 'Don't you worry, you'll see
Spike again – very soon,' said Sam.

Lauren looked at Sam. 'Didn't you catch a jewel robber recently?'

'I certainly did,' replied Sam, swelling with pride. 'The police had been after him for years, but it took me to track him down.'

Ella, standing beside him, coughed loudly and indignantly. Sam seemed to have totally forgotten he didn't catch this thief on his own.

But now Lauren was gazing at Sam really hopefully. 'If anyone can get Spike back for me, it's you.'

'That's true,' said Sam. 'Now, what I need . . .'

'Yes?' said Lauren eagerly.

'Have you got a dog whistle that Spike knows?'

'Yes, I have,' cried Lauren, digging into

her pocket. 'Here it is. He knows this whistle so well and always barks when he hears it.' Lauren's lip started to tremble again.

'Could I borrow it?' asked Sam.

'Of course.'

Sam took the whistle. 'And, don't worry, just leave it all to me.' He grinned at her, still not noticing Ella frowning beside him.

On the way home, though, Ella snapped. 'So you found the jewel thief all on your own, did you?'

'No, of course not . . . you helped.'

'Oh, thank you. So why didn't you mention that little fact to Lauren?'

Sam really had meant to say something, but somehow the words had just got stuck in his throat. He said quickly, 'Don't go on about that – the main thing is that we find Spike.'

'And how exactly are we going to do that?'

Sam stopped and grinned at her. 'I've got it all worked out. The park keeper said the man who'd stolen Spike practically ran out of the park. He didn't get into a car either. So that means the man probably doesn't live very far away. He might even be living in one of those houses right next to the park. So, this evening, you and I will walk around there blowing on the dog whistle, and, if Spike is anywhere nearby, he'll answer, won't he?'

'But will we hear him?' asked Ella. 'He could be locked away somewhere.' Then she stopped. 'Oh, I get it, we wouldn't

normally hear Spike, but if we go
online . . .'

'. . . then our supersonic hearing will
pick up Spike's tiniest cry. Now go on,
admit it, that's a great idea,' interrupted
Sam.

'Well, it might be,' said Ella cautiously.
They'd reached the Jolly Roger and she
gazed up at the hotel. 'But our lovely
uncle and aunt will never let us go out
tonight.'

'They won't be able to stop me,' said
Sam. 'Come on.'

WHERE IS SPIKE NOW?

Shock in
the Kitchen

Patch fell on the twins as if he hadn't seen them for years. (In fact, most lunchtimes one of the twins came back to take him for a walk.) He yelped with happiness, and licked them madly.

Then Aunt Joy announced from the doorway, 'That dog is going to have to go.'

'But after we found the jewel thief

you promised Patch could stay with us,' cried Ella.

'We never actually promised,' said Aunt Joy. 'We said we'd see how he behaved himself.'

'No, you didn't,' said Ella.

'If Patch goes, I'll go too,' said Sam.

Aunt Joy looked quite unmoved by this threat. 'That dog's nothing but a big nuisance. He howls for ages after you've gone, then he races about the hotel getting under everyone's feet.'

'He'll learn,' begged Ella. 'Give him a chance.'

'Well, he's running out of chances,' sighed Aunt Joy. 'All he does is cause me more work.'

'But he loves you, don't you, Patch?' said Ella.

Patch, who'd been leaping so enthusiastically over Ella and Sam, just stared at Aunt Joy, his tail not wagging even a tiny bit.

'A dog's been stolen, Aunt Joy,' said Sam. 'I said we'd put up this poster in case anyone has seen it.'

Aunt Joy's long, pinched face frowned. 'All this fuss over a mangy dog,' she sniffed.

'We're going to see if we can find him later,' Sam went on.

'Oh no, you're not,' said Aunt Joy. 'For the first time in weeks we're full up. In fact, just for tonight the restaurant is so busy we can't fit everyone in.' She rubbed her hands together excitedly. 'We've got to have two sittings. And you'll be kept very busy with all the washing up.'

'Aunt Joy, would you mind doing the washing up, just this once?' asked Ella. 'We wouldn't ask normally but we're trying to find a stolen dog who's probably feeling very scared . . .'

'How dare you!' rumbled a voice behind Aunt Joy. Uncle Mike's huge, bloodshot eyes blazed at Sam and Ella. 'I've been out since eight o'clock this morning handing out flyers to try and get us some more customers. We need them because you two are costing us a fortune. And how do you repay us? With rudeness and cheek! Well, neither of you is to step one foot out of this hotel tonight. Is that clear?'

Neither Sam nor Ella answered him at first.

'Is that clear?' he thundered.

'Yes,' whispered Ella.

'Yes,' whispered Sam, even more faintly.

'Now forget everything else and go and start your kitchen duties,' said Uncle Mike. 'You're already very late.'

Patch, not liking the way Uncle Mike was talking to Sam and Ella, gave a low growl.

'And keep that dog out of my way,' snapped Uncle Mike, 'or you'll be very sorry.' He lumbered away, still muttering about the twins.

'Now see what you've done,' screeched Aunt Joy, and she went flapping after him.

'They spoil everything,' cried Ella. 'And they couldn't care less about Spike.'

'Well, I'm still going to find him tonight,' said Sam, 'and I don't care what they do to me.'

'I wish there was some way we could get our chores over with really quickly,' began Ella. 'You don't suppose we could use our special powers so we can work twice as fast?'

'What an incredibly brilliant idea,' cried Sam. 'And why ever didn't I think of it?'

They charged down to the kitchen and, after leaving Patch outside with a bone, they quickly got online.

The dishwasher was broken (it had been for several days) so Sam and Ella had to do all the mountains of washing up by hand. But today it was brilliant fun. Plates and cups were washed and dried before the twins knew what was happening. The best bit of all was putting the dishes away, though. They just sprang out of Sam's hands and dived on to the shelves. Never had plates, forks and spoons moved so fast.

Then it was Ella's turn. She laughed in delight and exclaimed, 'You've only got to give the tiniest tap to a plate and it just hurls itself away. And look how quickly we're getting everything done . . .'

Suddenly down her ear she heard Sam shout, 'Stop! Stop now.' His voice sounded so anxious she froze.

Then she slowly looked round and saw Aunt Joy blinking and gulping at her.

Whistling for Spike

Ella glanced at Sam in dismay. The very last thing they'd wanted was for Aunt Joy and Uncle Mike to discover their secret powers. Aunt Joy didn't speak at first. She just stood there with her mouth wide open. Then she gasped and gurgled and snorted, but speaking was still beyond her.

Ella stepped forward, smiling innocently. 'Hello, Aunt Joy, how's things?'

Aunt Joy finally managed to splutter, 'What . . . what is going on here?'

Ella, still smiling innocently, asked, 'Whatever do you mean, Aunt Joy?'

'The way you two were moving about,' cried Aunt Joy. 'It was as if you were all speeded up somehow.'

'I'm very sorry,' said Ella, 'but I don't understand what you mean. Do you, Sam?'

'Haven't a clue,' said Sam at once. 'Very sorry.' Then they both smiled politely at her.

Aunt Joy's eyes stretched even wider. 'But I saw . . .' she began. Then she plonked down on a chair. 'Get me a glass of water,' she demanded. She gulped down the water so fast that she let out a giant burp.

Ella put a hand over her mouth to stop herself from bursting out laughing.

'I've been working far too hard,' spluttered Aunt Joy, 'that's what it is . . . and now my eyes are playing tricks on me. Tell your Uncle Mike I'm going to rest for a while.' Then she staggered out.

Sam said to Ella, 'That was quick thinking.' He grinned. 'Did you hear that massive burp Aunt Joy let out?'

'They heard that two hundred miles away,' said Ella.

They both fell about giggling, until Sam declared, 'Well, we've put away every single knife, fork, spoon and plate – so let's go and find Spike now.'

And they were both in such good spirits they completely forgot there were two sittings in the restaurant that night.

They sped out of the hotel, with Patch gambolling excitedly beside them. It was drizzling with rain now and had got dark quite early, but Ella and Sam hardly noticed. They were still laughing about Aunt Joy when they reached the row of houses nearest the park.

'Time to go online again,' said Sam.

They both closed their eyes and concentrated. A few seconds later they heard that familiar humming noise. A ripple of electricity rushed up Ella's spine. Life was changing into something magical.

No one could ever guess all the super powers she and Sam now possessed, thought Ella. Why, they could even hear what people were saying inside their houses – that's how strong their hearing was now.

They eavesdropped on one boy and girl having a massive row. 'Never, ever go in my bedroom again – it's private!' the girl screamed.

'Oh, just shut up and rest your brain,' the boy cried back.

Sam grinned. 'They're worse than you and me when we argue.'

'Oh, we haven't had a row like that for ages,' said Ella. 'And that's the way I like it,' she added softly.

'So do I,' Sam replied, even more quietly. Then he took out the dog whistle. 'Now Spike knows this whistle very well and we've got to listen out for his bark, which Lauren says is more like a yap really.'

He blew the whistle and then, to their total amazement, they heard a sleepy, muffled yap.

'That's Spike,' cried Sam. 'And he sounds half asleep. I bet that's because he's been drugged. He can hardly bark at all really, but our mega hearing picks up his little yelps.' He looked at Ella. 'So, what about that? – we've found Spike already. He's in there.' He pointed at the rather rundown house in front of them.

'But why keep Spike drugged in there?' asked Ella.

'I'll tell you why,' said Sam. 'They're going to send a note to Lauren's dad saying they've got Spike and, if he wants him back, he's got to pay them a ransom.

They'll probably ask Lauren's dad to leave the money under an oak tree at midnight – that's what dognappers usually do.'

'How mean is that!' cried Ella. Then she asked, 'So what are we going to do?'

'We could ring up Lauren's dad . . .' Sam began, but then he shook his head. 'No, let's get Spike out of there ourselves. I bet I could fight all the dog snatchers.'

'Exactly how many do you think there are?' asked Ella anxiously.

'Oh, there's probably a whole gang in there,' said Sam airily, 'but they don't frighten me. Don't forget, we're mega strong now.' And he started walking down the drive.

'Shouldn't we think about this a bit more?' Ella called after him.

'No,' said Sam, and before Ella knew

what was happening he'd already rung the doorbell. He turned round to her. 'Why are you waiting back there?'

'Because I . . .' began Ella.

But there was no time to say anything else. The door had already opened.

Sam's Mistake

A sharp-faced woman peered suspiciously at them. 'Yes?' she demanded.

'Have you got a dog here?' asked Sam sternly, and without waiting for a reply he yelled, 'Spike, come on, boy! Spike!' Then he got out his whistle and started blowing on it.

The woman stared at Sam as if he were mad. 'Whatever is he doing?' she asked Ella, who was hovering behind him.

And then they heard a dog give a little yelp. 'That's Spike,' cried Sam at once.

'Who's this Spike?' The woman continued addressing all her questions to Ella.

'We need to see your dog,' said Ella; then she added politely, 'if you don't mind.'

'No, I don't mind,' said the woman. She opened the kitchen door and an elderly spaniel shuffled forward, his tail swishing slowly behind him. He gazed mournfully around, then spotted Patch and gave another very sleepy yelp.

'This is my dog,' the woman said proudly. 'He's fourteen years old, that's ninety-eight in dog years.'

'He's marvellous,' said Ella. 'And we're very sorry to have bothered you.'

The woman leant forward and hissed to Ella, 'I'd take him home, if I were you.' Sam was too busy turning bright red to reply.

After the woman had closed the door Sam looked as deflated as a burst balloon. He waited for Ella to go on about how his plan had totally messed up and they'd found the wrong dog. But she just said, 'Never mind, let's try the next house.'

Sam blew his whistle again. This time a black Labrador jumped up at the window and started howling. And then Patch joined in the howling too.

'The trouble is, every dog can hear that whistle,' said Ella. 'And so . . .'

'Yeah, all right,' he snapped. 'It was a

very stupid idea, I know.' He put the whistle away and sighed loudly.

At that moment a car pulled up. 'Hello there,' said a familiar voice. It was Lauren's dad. Sitting beside him was Lauren. 'We're having a drive around,' he said, 'just in case we happen to spot Spike somewhere.'

'Any luck yet?' asked Lauren, smiling hopefully at Sam.

He lowered his head. 'No, not yet,' he mumbled.

'Well, it's a bit late for you two to be out now,' said Lauren's dad. 'Jump in and I'll give you a lift home.'

Sam, Ella and Patch scrambled into the back of the car. Ella did all the talking. Sam just sat there, looking extremely fed up.

After they'd been dropped off at the
Jolly Roger Sam said, 'I don't want to go
in yet. Let's take Patch for a bit of a run
around first.' Darkness seemed to have
settled over everything. And it was
raining quite hard now. But Ella didn't
argue.

The tide was out so the beach seemed
really huge. Sam pulled a ball out of his
pocket, and Patch began to dance about,
barking excitedly. Sam threw the ball as
far as he could. Patch tore after it. 'Come
on, bring it back to me,' cried Sam. But
Patch hadn't quite grasped this part of
the game yet. He just stood with the ball
in his mouth, wagging his tail wildly.

So in the end Sam raced over to him
and threw the ball further down the
beach. Patch galloped away. Sam smiled

until he heard a voice bellow out of the
darkness.

'What on earth do you think you are
doing? Come here at once.'

Sam whirled round and saw Uncle
Mike. He rushed back. He and Ella stood
very close together while Uncle Mike
roared, 'How dare you both just run
away! We had two sittings tonight.'

'Oh no,' groaned Ella, 'we totally
forgot about that. We're very sorry.'

'You forgot!' cried Uncle Mike,
quivering angrily while rain dripped
down his face. 'Do you have any idea
how busy we've been tonight? Well, all
the dishes have been left for you, and
you'll have to wash them up now.'

'That's fine,' said Ella hastily. 'We'll
clean them all.'

'Of course you will. What a busy night it's been for me, especially with your aunt having to rest all evening.'

All at once Sam remembered Aunt Joy's face earlier that evening and let out a loud laugh. He just couldn't help it.

This made Uncle Mike roar furiously, 'Go back to the hotel NOW, you useless boy, or I'll lock you out for the night!'

Sam knew he would as well. And it wasn't quite the weather for sleeping on the beach, so he scrambled hastily after Uncle Mike, calling to Ella to get Patch.

'I've a few more things to say to you about your attitude, young man,' shouted Uncle Mike. Sam sighed and settled in for a big lecture. He had just reached the hotel when a buzzing sound started up in his ear. This was a signal that Ella was trying to get a message to him. He cleared his mind and instantly heard a low, very wobbly voice.

'Sam, I can't find Patch.'

The Dog Snatcher
Strikes Again

When Ella couldn't find Patch she immediately began to tremble. But then she took a deep breath and told herself she must somehow keep calm — and think out what to do.

First of all she had to go online. She stood listening intently for that buzzing noise that meant she was getting through. Immediately a new strength flooded through Ella. She was still talking to Sam when she saw a man on the cliffs. She called up to him. He looked round for a moment: a man in a big, bulky coat.

Ella just wanted to ask him if he'd seen Patch. But instead the man started rushing away. This was highly suspicious behaviour, she thought. And Sam agreed.

So Ella went after him, her heart beating furiously. The man was running quite quickly now, but she shot off like an arrow behind him. She'd never run this fast before – no wonder she felt giddy – but she was catching up.

Suddenly he glanced round. He had a cap right down over his face so she couldn't see him very well at all. But he wasn't anything like the man the park keeper had seen – being very short and rather plump.

Ella was sure he was carrying Patch under his jacket. 'Patch, can you hear me?' Ella shouted.

And her sharp hearing caught Patch's muffled bark.

At the same time she could hear Sam urging her on: 'Run faster! Faster!' She felt very dizzy indeed now, as if she were on a merry-go-round that wouldn't stop. And she was gasping, not because she was out of breath, but because her stomach had turned upside down.

'Stop!' screamed Ella at the man. 'Dog snatcher! Stop!' And she heard Patch barking again, as if telling her to hurry up and save him.

All at once the man was just in front

of Ella. She went flying towards him and her hand shot out. She'd just meant to tap him on the shoulder, but she'd forgotten her colossal strength right now. One push of her hand was enough to send the man reeling forward with a cry of shock.

He fell down, groaning. Patch, seeing his chance, scrambled out of his grip and dashed over to Ella. She picked him up and hugged him very hard, while the man stumbled to his feet and, without looking back, half ran, half limped away.

Ella crouched over as if she had stomach ache. The speed at which she'd been running had made her feel quite sick, but what did that matter now that she had Patch back? She quickly told

Sam, 'It's all right. I've got Patch again,'
and cheering erupted in her right ear,
while Patch was licking her face madly.

Sam said he'd do all the washing up by
himself so Ella could look after Patch.
She carried the little dog into her
bedroom and then put him down gently
on the floor. But he didn't run about as
usual. Instead he looked at her and
started to shake.

'Oh, you really didn't like being
dognapped, did you?' cried Ella. 'I'm not
surprised.' Patch had his own basket, but
tonight, so that he could smell Ella's
scent and know that he was completely
safe, she let him sleep on her bed.

He curled up beside her pillow.
'Nothing bad's ever going to happen to

you again,' said Ella, stroking him. 'I'll see to that.'

Finally, Sam appeared from his marathon washing-up session. He crouched down and picked up a very sleepy Patch, while Ella started telling him in more detail what had happened. She was feeling rather proud of herself until Sam had to spoil it all by saying, 'So you didn't get a proper look at this dog snatcher? You let him get away from you.'

'Well, he wasn't the very tall, bald man Mr Westbury saw at the park. He was quite short . . .'

'There's a gang of them all right,' interrupted Sam. 'Shame you didn't see his face, though.'

'Oh, sorry,' said Ella indignantly, 'but

that's very difficult when he's wearing a cap – and it was dark!'

'If I'd been there, I wouldn't have let that dog snatcher get away,' Sam went on. 'No, I'd have captured him.'

'Well, at the time,' replied Ella, 'I was much more worried about Patch.'

'I'm only saying you could have saved Patch *and* caught the dog snatcher.'

'As you would have done,' cried Ella.

'Of course.'

'Well, sorry to disappoint you, but I was feeling a bit sick from running so fast. I've never run like that in my life before. Also, I was very giddy.'

'No, it's OK, you did your best,' said Sam in such a patronizing voice that Ella wanted to hit him.

Then he asked, 'Can you say anything

else about this man you saw, apart from that he's short and fat?'

'He had a long grey coat on and new black boots . . . I do remember noticing those.'

'Well, that's just great,' muttered Sam. 'We'll spend all our time staring at people's feet.' He sighed. 'I've got to do something. I mean, I can't just stay here and go to bed. I want to go out and catch all these dog snatchers.'

'So Lauren will think you're wonderful,' teased Ella.

'No, of course not,' said Sam, going red.

'I believe you, beetroot features.'

Sam gave Patch a last stroke before storming off. He hadn't liked her saying that about Lauren at all, thought Ella.

Well, good. He deserved it after spoiling tonight. Fancy saying he'd have caught the dog snatcher as well! Sam could be such a show-off sometimes.

Sam Makes
a Promise

Next morning Ella and Sam were still pretty unfriendly with each other. But all their disagreements were forgotten later when something dramatic happened at school.

David was a year younger than Ella and Sam, but Sam knew him quite well as they were in the same school football team. Only, David wasn't at football training after school that day. And Sam soon found out why. David had a West Highland terrier called Jessie. She was a great dog – very friendly. And now she too had been stolen.

David's mum had just left her tied up outside the post office for a couple of minutes while she popped in to get some stamps. When she came out all that was left was the lead – the dog had gone. No one had seen anything either. Jessie just seemed to have vanished.

Later that evening Sam slipped away to see David and his family. David looked dazed and lost. 'Jessie was the best dog in the world,' he said. 'And I'm never going to see her again.'

'Yes, you are,' said Sam. 'We'll track this gang down.'

David's mum nodded. 'That's the spirit. We've got to stay hopeful.'

David's family had also made some posters. They'd even offered a reward of £300 to anyone who could help them find Jessie. 'I know it sounds like a lot of money,' said David's mum, 'but Jessie is like a member of the family . . . and we'll do anything to get her back.'

Next day there was a big article in the local paper about the dog thefts. People were urged to keep a close eye on their dog.

Meanwhile every night Lauren and her dad walked around Little Brampton, just to check Spike wasn't lying hurt or injured somewhere. They carried on asking people if they'd seen Spike too.

But no one ever had, even though posters of the two missing dogs were everywhere, including all over the Jolly Roger. Uncle Mike went mad when he saw them and promptly ripped them down.

'He just doesn't care,' said Sam, pacing up and down Ella's bedroom. He sighed heavily. 'He hasn't even left one poster up, and those dog snatchers are still out there – but where? I was hoping there might have been a ransom note by now. Then I could have lain in wait for the gang to pick up their money – and overpowered them all.'

'Single-handedly, of course,' said Ella.

'Oh, I might have asked you to come along too.'

Ella smiled. 'You're so kind.' Then she said, 'We need some clues.'

'We haven't got any,' said Sam, 'except for the fact that one of the dog snatchers was wearing new black boots . . . and a lot of good that is.'

'All right,' said Ella, 'don't start on that again.' She paused. 'We could go along and interview Mr Westbury and see if he can remember anything else about the dog snatcher at the park.'

'I suppose we could,' said Sam unenthusiastically. 'Yeah, all right then.'

But it was while interviewing the park keeper that they discovered a very important clue.

A Very
Important Clue

Next day, before school started, Sam and Ella went to see Mr Westbury. Just inside the park was a cafe. Mr Westbury was setting out the tables when they found him. He took them to his office, which was about the size of a car boot. There were posters of Spike and Jessie all over one window. And underneath them one advertising the Jolly Roger. Mr Westbury said he'd been expecting Sam and Ella, which made them feel rather important.

'Lauren's dad told me you two were investigating this case,' he said. 'You're the ones who found that jewel thief, aren't you?'

'Yes, that's right, *we* did,' said Ella, darting a glance at Sam.

'I remember reading about that in the local paper,' Mr Westbury said. 'So have you got any clues as to the dog snatcher?'

'Yes,' said Ella, 'but we'd like some more. That's why we need you to tell us again what happened the morning Spike was stolen.'

'And don't miss out a single detail,' added Sam.

'Well, as you know, the man I saw was

bald and extremely tall.' Mr Westbury gave a little chuckle. 'Still, most people look tall to me.' He was very small and round. 'But I'd say he was well over six foot, a fast walker all right . . . and, oh yes . . . shortly after the incident I found a handkerchief right by the scene of the crime. Of course I don't know for certain that it was dropped by the dog thief – but it's possible, isn't it?'

'It certainly is,' said Sam eagerly.

Mr Westbury leant forward. 'And right in the corner of the handkerchief were these tiny initials – M. R.'

'M. R.' repeated Sam. 'Well, they could be the dog snatcher's initials.'

'I think they are,' said Mr Westbury.

'Can we see the handkerchief?' asked Sam.

'It's rather dirty,' said Mr Westbury.

'Oh, a few bogeys don't bother me,' replied Sam.

'No.' Mr Westbury grinned. 'I mean it's a bit grubby, that's all.' Then he went over and brought out an expensive-looking blue handkerchief with the initials in black in the corner.

'He's obviously quite rich,' said Ella.

Sam asked, 'Could we borrow this handkerchief just for a day or two, please?'

Mr Westbury looked a bit doubtful.

'I really think this could be a significant clue,' said Sam.

'Well, the police don't seem at all interested in it,' said Mr Westbury. 'So, all right then . . . I'll put it in a little bag for you. And, if this helps track down our dog thief, well, I'll be very happy indeed.'

On the way to school Ella asked, 'Why on earth did you want to borrow that smelly handkerchief?'

'Ella, who do we know with those initials?'

His sister shrugged.

'And you're supposed to be the clever one – Uncle Mike, of course.'

Ella stopped walking and stared at Sam. 'You're not serious.'

'He's got the same initials. And the man Mr Westbury saw was very tall and bald. Well, Uncle Mike's very tall and could easily be mistaken for a boiled egg.'

'I still don't think he's the dog snatcher,' said Ella.

'I do,' said Sam firmly. 'And, don't forget, he has been away a lot recently.'

'Handing out flyers about the Jolly Roger,' said Ella.

'He could be doing that *and* stealing dogs,' said Sam. 'No, we should see if Uncle Mike recognizes this hankie. If he does – well, we've got one of the dog snatchers.'

Ella gasped.

Sam grinned. 'I've really shocked you with my amazing intelligence, haven't I?'

'Let's just say you've shocked me,' said Ella.

At school Sam even went up and told Lauren, 'I think I'm about to track down one of the dog snatchers.'

'Oh, but that's brilliant,' she cried, all excited, 'especially as the police say they haven't anything new to tell us.'

'Just leave it all to me,' said Sam.

10

News of
Mrs Rice

When they got back from school they saw Uncle Mike standing behind the reception desk at the Jolly Roger. He scowled at the two children. 'Can't you come into my hotel a little more quietly?'

'Sorry, Uncle Mike,' said Sam, sidling up next to him.

'I'm always having to remind you,' said Uncle Mike.

'I know, but from now on we'll tiptoe in and out of here. I promise,' said Sam. 'So how are the bookings?'

'Improving, no thanks to you,' grunted Uncle Mike.

Then Sam crouched down. 'Oh, by the way, you dropped this.'

Uncle Mike squinted at the blue hankie in Sam's hand while Sam and Ella waited breathlessly. Then he snatched it up. 'Hmm, so I did,' he muttered.

A little shiver ran up Ella's back. She didn't like Uncle Mike very much – but she'd never imagined him as a dog snatcher.

Then something really alarming happened. A hideous smile appeared on Uncle Mike's face out of nowhere, and he asked Sam, 'So, lad, did you have a good day at school today?' This total change of character could only mean one thing: Uncle Mike had spotted someone else coming into the hotel.

Sam turned and saw who it was – David with his mum.

'Guess what, Sam,' yelled David across the entrance. 'I think Jessie's been found.'

'What!' exclaimed Sam and Ella together.

David rushed on, 'This woman called Mrs Rice rang up, saying she's sure she bought Jessie at an agricultural show yesterday. She was a bit suspicious at the time but it was only today she saw one of our notices and recognized Jessie right away.'

'That's the best news I've heard for centuries,' cried Sam.

David grinned and nodded. 'She said we can call round any time after five o'clock today to collect Jessie and it's nearly that now . . . so we just wondered if you'd like to come with us.'

'*Would* we!' said Sam eagerly.

But then he remembered Uncle Mike, who normally would have snapped, 'No, of course you can't go – you've got far too much work to do here.' But in front of other people Uncle Mike had to put on a bit of an act, so he displayed all his brown teeth and said, 'Now I think it might be a bit crowded with both of you there, but, Sam, you certainly may go along.'

Ella tried hard not to look too disappointed. Sam whispered to her before he left, 'I'll tell you everything that happens.' She knew he would, but meanwhile Ella had to do her least favourite job: cleaning the kitchen floor.

'Can I go and see Patch first?' she asked.

'No, you can't,' snapped Uncle Mike, back to his usual self. 'That wretched dog started howling and yelping after you went back to school this afternoon. Well, he'd better behave himself tomorrow night.'

'Tomorrow night?' asked Ella.

Uncle Mike stamped his foot impatiently. 'How many times do I have to remind you? That's when we have all these important people coming to watch a film in the dining hall about the history of Little Brampton.'

'Oh yes, sorry – I'd forgotten,' whispered Ella.

'Well, if your germ-carrying mutt barks just once tomorrow, we're going to sell him.'

'Don't worry, he won't. He's a good dog really,' said Ella hastily.

Uncle Mike pulled the blue handkerchief with his initials on out of his pocket and proceeded to blow his nose very loudly. 'Wretched cold,' he muttered. 'Just can't shake it off.' Ella watched him, horrified. *So it really was his handkerchief that had been found at the crime scene.* She still couldn't believe it.

'What are you staring at?' demanded Uncle Mike suddenly. 'You haven't got time to stand gawping at me, especially as your aunt's got one of her headaches. Now get cleaning that kitchen floor.'

But, after he'd gone, Ella carried on wondering about Uncle Mike's secret life of crime. And then she heard a buzzing in her ear. She instantly cleared her mind and heard Sam saying triumphantly, 'So what about Uncle Mike admitting that hankie belonged to him? I was right, wasn't I?'

'Yes,' she agreed, 'you were.'

'This is to let you know what's happening. We found Mrs Rice. She lives in a cottage a little way on from the park. She's dead old and very smiley. And guess what – the dog is Jessie all right.'

'Oh, I'm really pleased,' cried Ella.

'Jessie went mad when she saw David. His mum is writing Mrs Rice a cheque now. She paid one hundred and fifty pounds for the dog and David's mum is insisting on paying her that back, as well as the three hundred pounds reward.'

'Wow,' gasped Ella. 'So she's getting a cheque for four hundred and fifty pounds.'

'But she said she's very sorry to say goodbye to Jessie, as her own dog died six months ago and she's been very lonely ever since.'

'I can imagine . . . still, with all that money she can buy another one,' said Ella.

'That's true. I'm going to ask Mrs Rice a few questions now.'

'Well, don't go offline,' said Ella. 'It's very lonely here on my own.'

'All right, I'll stay online . . . and keep you posted.'

And Sam did. He repeated everything

Mrs Rice had told him about buying the dog at the agricultural show. The person who'd sold Mrs Rice the dog did give her a phone number. But, of course, it was a false one.

'I wonder,' said Ella, 'how Jessie ended up at that agricultural show. Did the gang take her there?'

'Well, I suppose it's a good place to sell dogs,' said Sam. He added, 'And I bet the chief dog snatcher is Uncle Mike.'

'We need a bit more proof than one hankie,' replied Ella.

'And we'll get it,' said Sam, 'but now we're all leaving. Jessie and David have charged off into the car already. But David's mum is still talking to Mrs Rice at the door . . .' All at once Sam's voice stopped.

Ella actually tapped her ear. 'Sam, Sam
. . . are you still there?'

Then she heard Sam's voice again but
it sounded hushed and shocked.

'Ella, I've picked up a sound that
neither David's mum nor Mrs Rice have
heard. It was a high-pitched yelping. It
has to be Spike!'

Ella gasped. 'But where was it coming
from?'

Sam paused, and then said, 'From
Mrs Rice's garden.'

11

Patch in
Trouble

Later that night it looked as if Sam
and Ella were sitting in Ella's
room without saying a word to each
other. Certainly their lips didn't move
once. But, actually, they were talking
away like crazy. Sam had decided it was
too dangerous to even whisper about
the dog snatcher, now that Uncle Mike
was a top suspect. So they were talking
online.

Patch sat up and watched them with his black-and-white ears sharply pricked, as if he sensed something magical were going on.

Ella's ear was scalding hot tonight. In fact, it felt just as if it had sunburn. Touching it was really quite painful. She supposed this was because she'd been online so much with Sam lately.

Still, Sam's discovery could be a real breakthrough. He was convinced Mrs Rice's house was where they were keeping Spike.

'What I don't understand,' said Ella, 'is how the tall, bald dog snatcher Mr Westbury saw, or the short one I saw, fit in with Mrs Rice.'

'They're all members of this dognapping gang. And don't forget Uncle

Mike as well. I bet they have a secret hiding place where they plot which dog to steal next. I'd love to find out where they're meeting and send a poisonous snake in there that would . . .'

'Yes, all right,' interrupted Ella. Sometimes Sam got a bit carried away and needed bringing back to earth. 'But what are we going to do next?'

'Tomorrow night we've got to go to Mrs Rice's house and rescue Spike.'

'If it *is* Spike you heard.'

'I'm sure it's him this time,' said Sam firmly.

'And, once we've got Spike, we'll tell the police where we found him and then Mrs Rice will have to talk,' said Ella.

'And give the reward money back,' said Sam. 'Talk about cheeky – you steal the dog yourself, and then ring up to claim the reward for returning him.'

'There's just one problem with tomorrow night,' said Ella. 'Uncle Mike and Aunt Joy are putting on this big do . . .'

'Oh, that's right,' groaned Sam. 'So there's no way we can both disappear. But it's OK – I'll go on my own.'

'Oh yes, and why has it got to be you?' demanded Ella at once.

'Because,' began Sam, then he grinned. 'Well, because I'm just the best. Everyone knows that.'

'Ha, ha,' cried Ella, 'and ha, ha, again.'

In the end they flipped a coin; the winner could go and save Spike.

And Ella won.

Sam frowned. 'We did say the best of three?'

'No, we didn't,' said Ella gleefully. 'I win but, don't worry, I'll think of you often, doing all that lovely washing up.' Then she added, 'Keep an eye on Patch. Uncle Mike says, if he makes one sound tomorrow night, then he will have to go.' Suddenly Patch twitched in his sleep and gave a little groan.

'Don't worry,' said Sam, stroking Patch, 'I'll keep an eye on him all right.'

The following evening Sam took Patch for a long walk. Then he settled their dog in a basket just outside the kitchen with a nice juicy bone.

Uncle Mike and Aunt Joy had been

rushing about greeting all the guests.
They were all dressed up tonight.
Uncle Mike was wearing a stripy jacket,
which made him look like a walking
deckchair.

Then the speaker, Mrs Withers, arrived:
a large, confident woman with a voice
that boomed even through into the
kitchen, where Sam was busily setting
out trays of tea, coffee and biscuits for
the end of her talk. No one would know
that he was also talking away to Ella, as
they were already online.

Suddenly Sam heard a loud thumping
noise by his feet. He looked down to
see Patch, his tail beating excitedly
against the ground. He crouched down.
'Now you know you're not supposed
to be in here.' Then he noticed that

Patch had brought his ball in with him too.

'Sorry, I can't play with you right now,' he began. But Patch looked so hopeful of a game that Sam's heart melted and he hurled the ball into the reception area. This time, to Sam's delight, Patch not only retrieved the ball – but he brought it back to him. 'Clever boy, you're getting it at last! I knew you would.'

Sam threw the ball again. Patch went tearing after it, but this time he bounded into a man arriving in the doorway.

'I'm very sorry,' cried Sam, rushing forward. The man brushed himself down, then stared hard at Sam through large, thick glasses.

'I'm here for the talk. I hope I'm not too late.'

'No, no,' said Sam, 'I'll show you
where it is.'

Still brushing himself down, the man
followed Sam along the corridor. After
Sam had shown him inside, Patch gave a
loud bark.

'Hey, shh,' said Sam at once. 'What's
the matter anyway? And where's your ball
gone?' Then Sam realized what had
happened. 'Oh, that man must have taken
it by mistake. Well, don't worry, we'll get
it back afterwards . . . and don't you dare
bark again. OK?'

Meanwhile Ella had slipped out of the
Jolly Roger. She'd found Mrs Rice's
cottage at the end of a little cobbled
lane. It looked so calm and peaceful
with ivy growing all over it. *Could*

Spike really be here? She took Spike's whistle out of her pocket and blew it right outside the cottage. At once there came a faint, faraway yelp, which she'd never have heard if she hadn't been online.

Now she too was certain that it was Spike. Her heart thumped excitedly. She was all set to rescue Spike right away. There was just one problem: Mrs Rice was standing in her doorway chatting with another woman. So there was no way Ella could slip past her and investigate the back garden at the moment.

'Don't worry,' said Sam when she told him, 'just stay online and be ready for your chance.'

Sam was about to say something else

when he heard a sound that made him freeze with horror.

It was Patch.

And he was barking very loudly and very angrily.

Ella to
the Rescue

Sam thought his head would explode.
Uncle Mike and Aunt Joy would
never forgive Patch for making all that
noise. Sam charged over to the dining
hall. The little man with large glasses
who'd arrived late clearly wanted to leave
early as well. But he couldn't because
Patch was dancing around his ankles and
barking furiously.

Uncle Mike strode out of the dining

hall, his face twisting with fury. 'We can't hear a word in there,' he said. 'What's the meaning of this racket?'

Sam opened his mouth, but not a word came out. And then a woman burst out of the dining hall. 'My purse has been stolen!' she shrieked. 'And I think you know something about it,' she cried, pointing at the man with the large glasses.

He tried to dart away but Patch began barking madly at him again. Other people were now spilling out of the dining hall, telling each other about things they'd had stolen – so this man had been busy creeping about in the dark, helping himself to anything he could find!

Aunt Joy rushed off to call the police

while Mrs Withers said in her booming voice, 'That dog of yours has saved the day. If it hadn't been for him, this scoundrel would have got clean away.'

There were murmurs of agreement and even Uncle Mike had to splutter, 'Yes, he's a good dog all right.'

After the police had taken the man away and everyone was going back into the hall, Uncle Mike whispered to Sam, 'You can give that dog, er . . .' He struggled to remember his name.

'Patch,' prompted Sam.

'Yes, you can give Patch some extra water tonight.'

'You're so generous,' muttered Sam. Then he gave Patch a massive hug. 'And you're so clever.' Of course, Sam wasn't completely sure if Patch had barked at the man because he knew he was a thief or because the man still had his ball. It was probably a bit of both, Sam decided. Anyway, Patch was a hero now, all right.

Sam told Ella everything that had happened, and then she hissed, 'Mrs Rice has finally gone inside – so it's up to me now.'

'You'll be great,' said Sam unexpectedly.

This gave Ella that extra little burst of confidence as she crept round to the back gate. It was padlocked and it was very high. Normally she wasn't at all keen on climbing but now that she was online she seemed to get up and over it in seconds. She felt a little glow of pride about that.

Then she looked around her. Although

Mrs Rice's cottage wasn't very big, her back garden was huge. It seemed to stretch out forever. And right at the bottom of the garden, dwarfed by all the trees surrounding it, was one lone shed.

Ella got out the whistle and gave a little blow. Right away a faint high-pitched yelp came from the shed. She'd found Spike. But Ella knew she mustn't get too excited yet. She still had to get him out without attracting Mrs Rice's attention.

So, slowly and carefully, she made her way down the garden. Every footstep she took sounded deafening to her. And it took a while edging down such a long garden but Ella didn't want to ruin anything now by getting over-hasty.

At last she reached the shed. There

were no windows, but she could hear the dog scratching at the door. 'Don't worry, Spike,' she whispered. 'I'll get you out.'

'What's happening? Come on, tell me everything,' demanded Sam in her ear.

'I've found Spike.'

'I knew you'd do it,' yelled Sam.

'I've just got to get him out of the garden now.' And then Ella heard another voice calling out.

'Who's there? Come on – show yourself. I'm not afraid.' It was Mrs Rice. Ella stopped dead. Mrs Rice walked around her garden, but luckily she didn't come as far as the shed. Finally, still muttering, she walked back inside. Ella heaved a great sigh of relief.

She waited a few seconds, and then she heard Spike whimpering inside the shed. 'Don't worry, I haven't forgotten you,' she whispered. Ella saw the shed was locked with a great, fat padlock. So no chance of opening that.

There was only one thing to do. 'I'm just going to have to smash my way into the shed,' she told Sam.

'All right,' said Sam. 'Now take your time; don't panic.'

Ella took a breath, then closed her eyes and ran at the shed. But at the last moment she swerved away. She just lost all her confidence.

'Have you done it yet?' asked Sam.

'Not quite,' she replied.

This was silly. She was super powerful now and she could ram that door open. Why couldn't she believe that?

Ella took another run. 'You can do

this,' she whispered to herself. And this time she didn't hesitate. She charged right at the door. It gave a splintering, cracking sound. And then the door just flew open. It was a fantastic moment.

Ella wasn't even out of breath. She gaped in amazement at what she'd done. Then she saw a little dog cowering in the corner of the shed. It *was* a corgi, but Lauren had described Spike as quite chubby – this dog looked pitifully thin to Ella. And Spike was supposed to be very lively; the small dog just stared anxiously at her. Maybe the poor thing had been drugged. She picked him up gently. 'Are you Spike or another stolen dog altogether? I'm not sure. But it's not right you should be kept in here, you poor little thing. I bet you're hungry as well.'

Then Ella stealthily began the journey out of the huge garden. She kept close to the fence. She just hoped Mrs Rice hadn't heard the shed door being smashed open. It was a very long way from the cottage.

At last Ella saw the back gate in front of her. Once she opened that she and this dog could escape from here forever. 'So far, so good,' she said to Sam. But then something shot out of the deep shadows by the gate. Ella couldn't even make out what it was at first. Her stomach lurched, terrified. Then she realized it was a very long stick. And holding it, right in front of her as if it were a gun, was Mrs Rice.

'What do you think you're doing?' she demanded. The stick hovered right in front of Ella's face now.

'I'm not doing anything,' cried Ella, 'except rescuing a stolen dog.'

'What are you talking about? That's a little stray I've been looking after.'

'In a padlocked shed at the bottom of your garden? I don't think so,' said Ella.

'You're trespassing and I shall call the police,' said Mrs Rice.

'Go on then,' cried Ella.

Mrs Rice hesitated.

'Either call the police or let me go,' said Ella.

Mrs Rice lowered her stick, but, suddenly, she started talking very loudly. This was so Ella wouldn't hear the person creeping up behind her. Only

Ella, with her super hearing, did realize someone was moving towards her. She whirled round defiantly, the dog in her arms.

But then she saw who the person was and gave a gasp of total shock.

Finding the
Dog Snatchers

'Mr Westbury,' gasped Ella, as she recognized the little park keeper. 'What on earth are you doing here?'

He took a deep breath and said quickly, 'Well, Mrs Rice asked me to look in. She'd found a stray dog roaming about the streets and wondered what she should do with it.'

'It's not a stray,' said Ella. 'It's a stolen

dog. I think it's Spike.' She clutched the poor little dog even tighter.

'Oh, I don't think so,' said Mr Westbury. 'But let's go inside and talk about this.' His voice was so reasonable and calm. 'I'm sure we can sort this out. Why don't you make us a cup of tea, Mrs Rice?'

'Of course I will,' said Mrs Rice, twinkling at Ella now. 'I think we all need to calm down, including me. It's just I get so worried about intruders. But don't worry, dear, I shan't file a complaint against you for trespassing.'

They were both acting so nice and friendly. But as Mr Westbury wiped his new black boots on the mat before strolling inside the house Ella gasped in amazement. She suddenly realized that he was the short plumpish figure she'd seen stealing Patch that night. Why hadn't she noticed that before? He even had on the same long grey coat.

So that other morning at the park there hadn't been any tall, bald thief. Mr Westbury had just made that up. No, he'd stolen poor little Spike himself. Then, when he heard that she and Sam were investigating the dog snatchers, he needed to send them on a totally false trail: he'd found Uncle Mike's handkerchief by chance and then pretended it had been dropped at the scene of the crime. Of course, he'd worked out who it belonged to and was certain she and Sam would as well.

Ella followed them through the back door of Mrs Rice's cottage. 'Take a seat, my dear. I'll make that tea,' said Mrs Rice, smiling at Ella, 'and I'm sure we can sort out this little misunderstanding.'

Ella heard Mrs Rice bustling about in the kitchen. She called out, 'Mrs Rice, this little dog could do with some water urgently.'

'Oh, of course,' she cooed, rushing in with a bowl of water.

Ella put the dog down. 'Go on then, have something to drink.' The little corgi gazed sleepily at her, wagged its tail weakly and then lapped up the water.

Inside the kitchen Mr Westbury and Mrs Rice were whispering, quite unaware that Ella, with her super powers, could hear every word.

Mr Westbury hissed, 'I don't like it.'

Mrs Rice replied, 'I know what I'm doing. This will give us time to think. Stupid little brat could ruin everything. What's she doing now?'

'Oh, she's just patting that dog that you said you'd look after,' Mr Westbury hissed back.

'And I *have*. It's not my fault if it won't eat anything I give it.'

'I knew we shouldn't have kept it here,' said Mr Westbury.

'Shut up moaning,' cried Mrs Rice, 'and leave it all to me.'

As well as listening to their whispered conversation Ella was also talking to Sam. 'Wow, I never, ever suspected Mr Westbury,' he said. 'Well, look, I'm going to call the police, so they should be there soon, but meanwhile be very careful. They're obviously planning to do something to you. Stay online.'

'Oh, don't worry about that – I will,' replied Ella. She felt a sudden welling of panic when Mrs Rice came clattering in with a tray of tea, smiling away.

Ella sensed danger very close to her now.

Danger!

Mrs Rice pulled up a little table and placed the tray on it. There were just two cups.

'Mr Westbury isn't a great tea drinker,' she explained. Then she added, 'Your cup is the one nearest to you.'

An idea burst into Ella's head. A moment later she looked round and pointed. 'Who's that in the garden?'

Both adults shot to their feet. They

even stepped outside for a few moments.
While they were away, Ella swapped
Mrs Rice's cup of tea with her own.

'I can't see anyone,' said Mr Westbury,
stomping back inside.

'Oh, sorry,' said Ella, 'I thought I saw a
shape rushing past the window . . . but
then I'm always imagining things.'

'Hmm.' Mrs Rice gave a grim little
smile and sat down slowly on the edge
of her chair. She picked up what had
been Ella's cup of tea and started
drinking quickly, as if to encourage Ella
to do the same. And all the time Ella
drank her tea she could sense them both
watching her intently.

Ella drained her cup. 'That was
delicious,' she said.

'My own special recipe,' said Mrs Rice,

with a dry laugh. Her eyes were still fixed on Ella. Mr Westbury's face was wet with sweat.

'So tell me how this little dog ended up at your house,' Ella asked Mrs Rice, wondering what lies she would cook up.

'Well, dear, I just found it roaming about in the fields one day, all by itself. I looked everywhere for its owner. No sign of anyone, so in the end I took it home.'

'And kept it locked up in a shed at the bottom of your garden,' said Ella.

'That was just to keep the little thing safe until I could consult Mr Westbury about what to do next. He's such a dog lover himself.'

Ella couldn't listen to these lies for another second. So, instead, she gave a little yawn. Instantly they both leant forward. Yes, this was what they had been waiting for.

'I'm sorry,' said Ella, 'I just feel so sleepy . . . you drugged my tea, didn't you?'

Mr Westbury said apologetically, 'Just a little sleeping draught. There'll be no harmful side effects. And it does give us time to disappear.'

'You are the dog snatcher, aren't you?' asked Ella.

It was Mrs Rice who replied. 'I'm the brains of this operation.' Her voice was quite different now, cold and boastful. 'He's just the muscle. He's also my nephew.'

Ella sat there looking from one to the other, gulping. 'How could you be so cruel as to steal dogs?'

A wild gleam came into Mrs Rice's eyes. 'Money,' she snapped.

'You'd be surprised how little a park keeper earns,' added Mr Westbury, a sulky, angry look now on his face.

'But that's no excuse for stealing people's dogs,' cried Ella, rage thumping inside her.

'Oh, if any owners offer big rewards we always try and reunite them with their dogs,' said Mr Westbury. 'That's why we still had Spike. We were sure his family would offer a reward soon.'

'And, if the owners don't, you just sell them on,' said Ella scornfully.

'After the fuss has died down, yes. Have a good refreshing sleep now, won't you, dear?' said Mrs Rice. She tried to get to her feet, but then gave a shocked gasp. 'I feel very strange,' she said.

Meanwhile Ella heard Sam say in her right ear, 'The police car is about to pull into the drive. How are you doing?'

'Just fine,' replied Ella. She sprang to her feet.

Mr Westbury and Mrs Rice gaped at her.

'Oh, sorry,' said Ella, 'did I not mention that I switched the teacups?'

Mrs Rice gave another strangled gasp.

'And the police are about to join us,' said Ella.

'The police!' echoed Mr Westbury.

'She's bluffing . . .' began Mrs Rice in an odd, slurred voice.

At that moment the doorbell rang.

'Shall I answer it as you're looking a bit sleepy?' said Ella to Mrs Rice.

Mr Westbury looked around desperately. Then he jumped up, put his head down and sprang towards the back door, obviously deciding to make a run for it. But Ella leapt forward and, not knowing what else to do, grabbed him by the shoulder. He shouted with surprise as she did so. She really didn't think she'd grabbed him very hard, but the effect was dramatic. He staggered and fell down with a big crash on to his chair again, clutching at his shoulder. He gazed up at her. 'How – how did you do that?' he spluttered.

'Oh, I eat my greens every day,' Ella smiled.

The doorbell rang again.

Mrs Rice was now snoring loudly and Mr Westbury was still looking dazed and very shocked, so Ella, with the corgi at her heels, opened the door to Sam and two policemen.

'You'll find the two dog snatchers in there,' she announced. 'One's a little injured and the other's fast asleep.'

15

*The Very Best
Part of All*

Later, when Sam and Ella talked about the end of the dog-snatching mystery, there were lots of good moments to remember.

Like the time they were interviewed by the local paper about how they helped defeat the dog snatchers. Patch had his picture taken too: the dog who trapped a thief.

All this publicity helped the Jolly

Roger get so many more bookings that Uncle Mike and Aunt Joy even smiled at the twins – once a week. Meanwhile, at school, a big fuss was made of Sam and Ella there. They even had to tell their story (missing out all the parts about their magic powers, of course) in assembly.

But both Sam and Ella agreed on what was the very best part of all. After Mr Westbury and Mrs Rice had been arrested, the twins took the little corgi round to Lauren's house.

They'd spoken to Lauren's dad first and said they weren't certain if this very miserable, very shy dog was Spike or not. So he'd told Lauren not to get her hopes up. She sat waiting anxiously for them up in her bedroom. Sam and Ella rushed inside. Sam was carrying the dog. 'This is who we found tonight. Could he possibly be yours?' he asked.

He let the dog down. Lauren stood staring at him for a moment, and then gave a cry of joy. The dog, weak as he was, wobbled towards her, yelping excitedly.

Lauren crouched down and gathered him up in her arms, her eyes looking as if they were about to pop out of her head. 'Oh, Spike, what have they done to you? It's all right now – you're home with me again. We'll soon feed you up.' Spike's tail gave a little flick at this news.

Lauren looked up. 'Oh, Sam, you did it! You rescued Spike, just as you said you would.'

'The dog snatchers really shouldn't

mess with me, you know,' began Sam. Then he looked at Ella and added hoarsely, 'I mean, *us*. Ella helped quite a bit too, by the way.'

'Well, thank you both so much,' whispered Lauren, tears racing down her face now, 'because this is, without doubt, the best moment of my entire life.'

As they left Sam whispered, 'I can't think of a better end to this adventure.'

And neither could Ella.

find out more about
PETE JOHNSON

If you were a superhero, what powers would you have and what would you be called?

I'd love to be able to run incredibly fast. That would be brilliant: speeding around, without any need to bother with cars or trains any more. Also, and this is embarrassing, I'd like to have super hearing, just like Ella and Sam. You see, I'm very nosy and . . . well, just think what I could find out! As for names: how about 'Mighty Pete'! Now, stop laughing . . .

Have you got a dog of your own?

Yes, she's called Tilly. A mad King Charles spaniel, who's three years old now but still thinks she's a puppy. I'm afraid she's not as well behaved as Patch. She's very excitable, especially if the doorbell rings; then she goes mad. But she's very affectionate and full of fun.

Do you have any brothers or sisters?

Yes, I have a younger sister called Linda. We both loved ghost stories and we even pretended our shed was haunted. One of us would sit inside the shed telling our friends scary stories. And the other would hide outside making strange, tapping noises on the window and even throw in a few ghostly groans. It was brilliant fun.

Where did you get the idea of the twins and talking online?

I've always been fascinated by twins – and especially the idea that one twin will always know when the other is in trouble. I interviewed some twins and then imagined what it would be like if you could secretly chat to your twin all the time.

What are you scared of? And how do you deal with it?

I've never liked the night very much and how it changes everything. Sounds are louder at night and your room grows somehow, doesn't it? But I've learnt to see that my fears really come out of my imagination and what I'm picturing in my head.

Which twin is most like you: Sam or Ella?

Sam, I'm afraid, especially when he does mad, crazy things and gets all carried away. That is very like me. But Ella is a great animal lover and so am I.

Have you ever met anyone as gruesome as Uncle Mike and Aunt Joy?

Happily no. But some of my teachers were quite scary. There was one who we nicknamed 'Bullet' and he was very bad tempered like Uncle Mike. He once gave a boy a double detention because he was breathing too loudly.

What was your favourite children's book?

I've got so many. Two favourites were *The House at Pooh Corner* by A. A. Milne – which I thought was better than *Winnie the Pooh*, even if the ending always made me sad – and *The Hundred and One Dalmatians* by Dodie Smith; friends would say, 'You're not reading that book again.' I still re-read it regularly.

What do you like doing best of all?

Being on holiday. And the very best thing of all is when you wake up on the first day of the holiday with it all stretching before you.

How did you become a writer?

I wrote a fan letter to Dodie Smith when I was eight. She wrote back and put the idea into my head of being a writer. She encouraged me to enter writing competitions. And when I was twelve I won ten pounds (wow!); it encouraged me and then I started writing more and more.

Visit Pete's official website at
petejohnsonauthor.com

Puffin by Post

2-Power: The Canine Conspiracy – Pete Johnson